What to Do? What to Do?

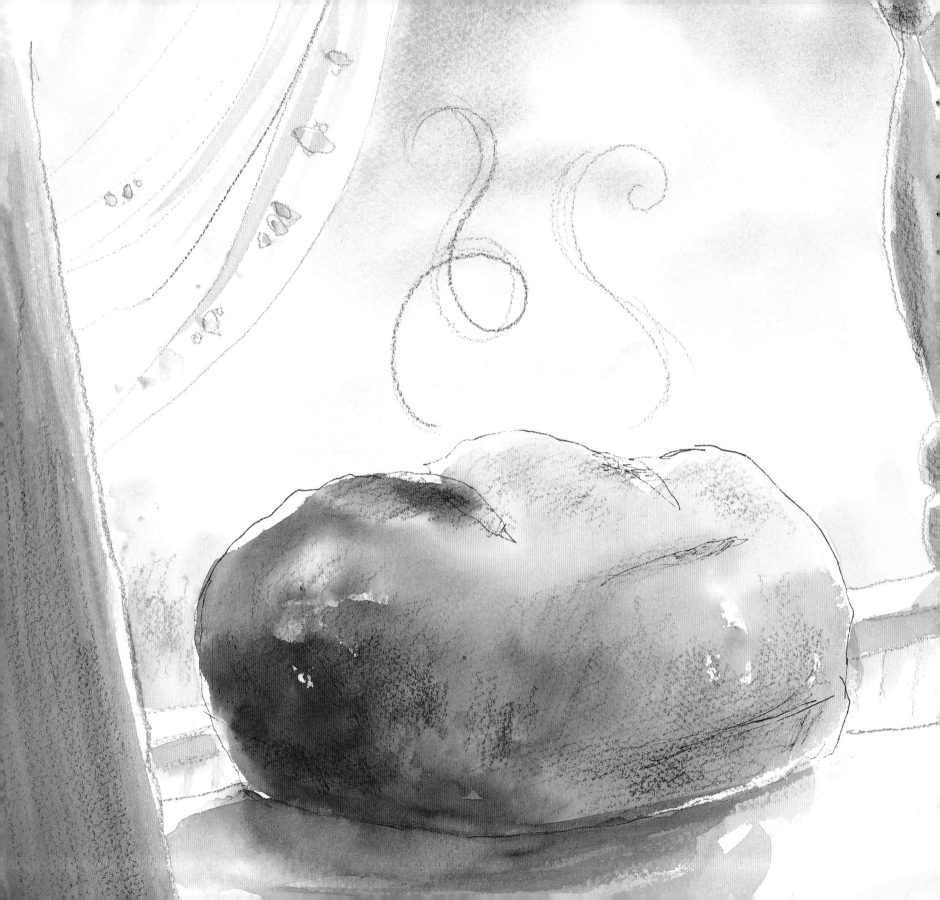

What to Do? What to Do?

by Toni Teevin
Illustrated by Janet Pedersen

Clarion Books

Clarion Books, a Houghton Mifflin Company imprint · 215 Park Avenue South,
New York, NY 10003 · Text copyright © 2006 by Etoile Strachota · Illustrations
copyright © 2006 by Janet Pedersen · The illustrations were executed in watercolor.
The text was set in 18.75-point Mrs. Eaves Roman. · All rights reserved. · For information
about permission to reproduce selections from this book, write to Permissions,
Houghton Mifflin Company, 215 Park Avenue South, New York, NY 10003.
www.houghtonmifflinbooks.com · Printed in China · *Library of Congress Cataloging-in-Publication
Data* Teevin, Toni. · What to do? what to do? / Toni Teevin ; illustrated by Janet Pedersen.
p. cm. Summary: Happy to have some companionship, Sophie bakes bread for visiting birds, but
finds she has a problem when they will not leave. · ISBN 0-618-44632-X · [1. Loneliness—Fiction.
2. Birds—Fiction. 3. Baking—Fiction.] I. Pedersen, Janet, ill. II. Title. PZ7.T22955 Wh 2006
[E]—dc22 · 2004022349

ISBN-13: 978-0-618-44632-2
ISBN-10: 0-618-44632-X

SCP 10 9 8 7 6 5 4 3 2 1

To my pride and joys,
with my unconditional love
—T.T.

For Joan
—J.P.

Old Sophie lived all alone. Her days were long and lonely. She talked to her cow. She talked to her cabbages. She talked to her pots, her pans, her flowers, her furniture. But, of course, she got no answer.

Every day, Sophie put on her bright orange hat and her shawl with the floppy fringe and went to the well for water. One morning, she saw birds nearby. "Nice birdies, sweet birdies," called Sophie.

And they seemed to call back! "Nice lady, sweet lady."

Sophie was delighted. All aflutter, she ran to the cottage. "I'll feed the dears!" she said.

Sophie baked bread as sweet as cake and as golden as the setting sun. She scattered crumbs all around and waited. The birds came flocking. "Nice lady, sweet lady," they twittered and tweeted. They perched on Sophie's shoulder and ate from her hand. Sophie loved it.

Sophie baked more bread.

The birds called their friends, and they came flocking. They sat on
Sophie's hat and squeezed onto her shoulders. They picked and pecked
and gobbled up every crumb.

Soon birds from all over knew the old woman who wore
the bright orange hat and the shawl with the floppy fringe.
But there was no more "Nice lady, sweet lady." They filled the
trees and lined the fence, screeching. They sat on the porch
and paced the roof, squawking. They crowded poor Sophie
and snatched and grabbed and quarreled over every morsel.

Sophie scolded them gently. "Now, now. No biting, no scratching, no shoving."

The birds paid no attention.

They filled the air with flapping wings and caws and hoots.

It was noisy, and there was never enough bread.

Sophie tried to keep the peace. She baked more and more, filling the air with a wonderful aroma. It floated over the countryside, all the way to the village. The people sniffed the air and smiled. "Who can be baking such sweet-smelling bread?" they asked one another.

Back at the cottage, Sophie had no smile. What she had was flour on her shoes, flour on her floor, and flour on her elbows. She was weary of kneading and baking, kneading and baking. But the greedy birds demanded more. *Screech, squawk, caw, hoot.*

What to do? What to do?

"Please, birdies," she pleaded, "no pestering. Please, birdies," she begged, "no shouting."

The birds paid no attention.

They followed Sophie everywhere.
They followed when she went to
milk her cow

and tend her garden.

They followed when she went to the village
for more flour.

"What to do? What to do?" Sophie
worried every step of the way.

When the people saw Sophie with her large sack of flour, one of them asked, "Do you bake the bread that fills the air with such sweet smells?"

"Yes," replied Sophie. "I bake bread for the birds."

"Would you bake bread for us, too?" asked a child.

Sophie looked up. The birds circled impatiently overhead.

"Sorry," said Sophie. "I can hardly keep up with the birds."

She hurried on her way.

And the birds followed.
What to do? What to do?

21

Shortly, Sophie saw a wagon coming down the road
with a sign that read:

TOO MANY PROBLEMS?
DON'T KNOW WHAT TO DO?
ASK VELMA
SEER, SAGE, AND CONFIDENTIAL ADVISER

Leaning from the wagon was Velma herself. "Tell your
fortune, good mother?" she crooned. "Solve your problems?
Step right in."

"I think I will," said Sophie.

Velma got right down to business. "What ails you, dearie? Warts? Corns? A nasty bee sting?"

"No," said Sophie.

"A lazy husband? A naughty child?"

"No," said Sophie.

"Well, what, then?" demanded Velma. "I haven't got all day."

Poor Sophie's words came out in a tumble. "Birds and bread, peck and shoo, squeak and squawk, what to do?"

Velma made no sense of it, but it didn't matter. "A terrible problem," she wailed. "Lucky for you, I'm a bird expert." To herself she thought, "I know a cuckoo when I see one."

"I will consult the crystal," she said importantly, peering into the glass ball. "Aha! The crystal says I need all your gold."

"But I have no gold," said Sophie.

"Then it says I need all your silver," said Velma.

"But I have no silver," said Sophie.

Velma was in a hurry. She banged on the table. "Well, what do you have?" she snapped.

Sophie looked at Velma. She did not see a seer. She did not see a sage. She did not see a confidential adviser. What she saw was a very greedy lady. Just like those birds, thought Sophie.

Right then, Sophie knew what to do.

"I have my beautiful orange hat and my shawl with the fine floppy fringe," said Sophie.

"It will have to do," Velma snarled. Just for show, she said a quick "hocus-pocus" and a hasty "alacazam." Just for show, Sophie listened.

Then Velma hustled Sophie out the door and snatched the hat and shawl. She climbed on her wagon, gave her mule a whack, and rode out of sight with her hat and fringe flapping.

ANY PROBLEMS?
KNOW WHAT TO DO?

And the birds followed.

As soon as Sophie heard the last caw and hoot, she picked up her sack of flour and hurried home. She went right to baking. She made pies, and cookies, and tarts, and sweet rolls, and, of course, her wonderful golden bread. Sophie hung a sign in the village:

ALL WELCOME FOR BAKED GOODS
MONDAYS AND FRIDAYS <u>ONLY</u>.
OTHER DAYS: STOP BY AND VISIT,
BUT BRING YOUR OWN BREAD.

31

How-do-you-do's were asked and told.
Tea was served and bread was sold.
Friends were made as good as gold.
And Sophie was never lonely again.